The Evergreen Wolf

Books by L. Sydney Abel

Gruvel the Great
Ish-ish Ishbochernay
Keypya and the Pirates
Kingsley Trunk
Marge and the Wobbly Onkey
Mr. Runkin's Secret
Patrick Duck
Smelly Nelly Welly
The Evergreen Wolf

The Evergreen Wolf

L. Sydney Abel

SPEAKING VOLUMES, LLC
NAPLES, FLORIDA
2018

The Evergreen Wolf

ISBN 978-1-62815-508-2

This book is for
Lindsay

Let your sky of stars shine upon this earth of ours

Thank you Karen for your patience and understanding

The characters in this book

MOONBEAM is a foolish pixie. I think to call someone foolish isn't nice, but you see, when someone has mischief written all over his face–as Moonbeam does–then foolishness is often the cause of his trouble. Moonbeam was all of a daffodil high. His round face and beaming smile gave him his name.

LILYBELL is also a pixie. We are all in some way brave. Lilybell was because she believed in Moonbeam. To understand, you have to be like Lilybell. She was what Moonbeam wasn't. That's not altogether correct. Moonbeam did have bravery, but his was in a foolish way. Lilybell was slender and just a smidgen shorter than Moonbeam. This ever-so-slight difference made Moonbeam think he was superior. I can tell you he wasn't, but it didn't stop Lilybell wishing to be taller. Sadly, wishes aren't meant for things like that. Besides, she was perfect just the way she was.

STRING is a soft toy dog and is longer than he is high; he'd been knitted from balls of string and then stuffed with goose feathers. He was just the right size to carry Moonbeam and Lilybell safely on his back. String owns two sewn-on eyes that are as black as coal and reflect everything.

Other characters are:

A MAGICAL OLD MAN
THE HERO
A RUBBERY THIEF
And, of course, THE LITTLE WOLF

A note:

The Rune Algiz, appearing as ψ in this story, is to do with wizard protection.

Algiz shows the antlers of an elk. It suggests the spreading fingers of a hand reaching up to the heavens in a protective gesture.

Algiz is a powerful rune of protection and spiritually it symbolises achievement in the pursuit of an adventure. A wizard's reading would be in knowing that the path ahead is full of danger—you should journey without fear, for the power of protection is inside you (you shall be safe if you refrain from being foolish).

The beginning

I had no doubt whatsoever in believing anything Mr. Hedges said. He had no reason to lie. I was told a story about a little wolf and two pixies.

This is what was said...

There is a wood where wolves and pixies live. Wolves hide by their colour. Their fur turns grey when winter brings its frostiness and then white when snow falls. It is only then that they climb the nearby hills to avoid Man, who comes into the woods to collect winter traditions.

Pixies have found a very clever way of hiding themselves, all due to a magical old man who reminds scatter-brained pixies about the danger of winter.

Table of Contents

Yan, tean, tither...

Possibly one of the most fascinating aspects of the York-shire dialect is the sheep counting rhyme/system that was traditionally used by shepherds.

There are lots of variations of course, all depending on where in the United Kingdom you come from.

Yan, tean, tither, mither, pip, teaser, leaser, catra, horner, dick, yan-dick, tean-dick...

Ages ago

Wizards can create anything. Now that you know this, it's easier to accept what follows...

There was once a wizard who stood in a wood and said:

'Let the sky of stars shine upon this earth of ours,
and let all its children be as colourful as flowers.'

What he meant by that was we should all be different in our own way. So before anything more is told, you must understand that being different is a good thing. Also, it's important to believe in pixies.

Yan

Moonbeam was holding a long, slippery worm and decided to tease Lilybell with it.

Lilybell hated worms. She screamed at the thought of a worm wriggling down the back of her neck. She ran out of the woods and into long grass that grew wild.

Moonbeam followed, his outstretched hand dangled the long, slippery worm just inches from Lilybell's slender neck. He was about to let go of the worm when he tripped, and then fell, unavoidably, flat on his face.

The worm wiggled free from Moonbeam's fingers, making a slippery escape.

Lilybell laughed and laughed until her sides ached.

Moonbeam didn't think it at all funny. He scowled from beneath a muddy face that blazed a throbbing nose. He looked to see what he had tripped over, and found a knitted dog lying in the long grass.

Lilybell liked the knitted dog so much that she called it String and decided to take it to the wizard, whose name was Ethelweard.

ψ

Bringing String to life with magic was the only way the wizard was sure to be left alone. He was far too busy with more serious works of magic to perform and so he granted Lilybell's pestering wish, just simply to get rid of her. Even wizards can be foolishly silly at times.

Ethelweard said:

"Duck feather within,

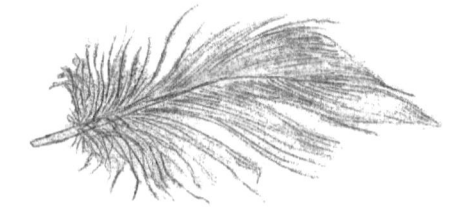

String feel like skin.

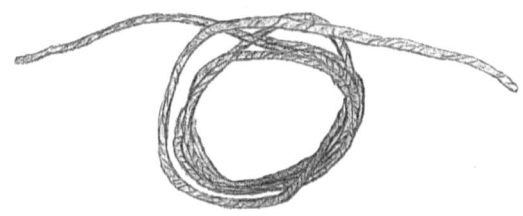

Eyes of coal see all,

let the wonder of life befall."

ψ

Moonbeam thought it his right, and his right alone, to name the place where String was found. He importantly decided on calling it 'the wild garden'. He also said it was to be their new and secret playground, and that they should only play there after midnight. Lilybell bravely agreed. String ran around as if he understood.

It was assumed–by all pixies–that after midnight, all people were fast asleep in their beds. Wizards knew differently.

Pixies weren't to be seen by anyone. Even though the woods were their home, they still had to be extremely careful not to be seen. They had to walk secret paths and never talk to any other creature that lived there, and that especially meant wolves. Wolves eat almost anything.

All the pixies had been told that wolves would eat them in a snap-bite second if it wasn't for the protective spell that had been cast over the woods.

If a wolf tried to eat any pixie, his teeth would crack and shatter; his claws would snap and splinter, and his tail would burst into flame and burn off.

Ethelweard thought the tail part was the best bit of magic he'd ever done (If you are wondering what this wizard looks like, well from what was told he's small and knobbly, not tall and straight like other wizards. He has what is standard to all his kind, a robe. Apparently he chose the colour himself. He was told he couldn't, but he did it anyway and picked black-or was it blue? But then again it might have been green. It varied constantly depending on the time of day. He was also three quarters of a millennium old).

There was a golden rule, and that was to never leave the woods' protection.

Moonbeam and Lilybell broke that rule. They shouldn't have, but adventure was hard to resist when it called on two naughty pixies.

On this particular night for playing, the moon was full and the sky was clear of cloud. This allowed every star to sparkle as brightly as it possibly could. Moonbeam, Lilybell and String walked towards the wild garden. As they walked, wolf eyes watched and wondered if dinner was coming their way.

Moonbeam and Lilybell got the better of the wolves; they jumped on String's back, who ran like the wind out of the woods and into the wild garden.

Tean

From the woods, eyes watched three friends at play. It was as if two small polished stones were reflecting the moonlight, for that was all that could be seen of the wolf.

The wolf crawled as low as possible to the ground. Then like mist, it left the trees. It moved silently through the undergrowth and lay in the tall grass.

Moonbeam, Lilybell and String didn't notice the wolf. They didn't notice the house, which the wild garden belonged to, had all its lights on. Strangely enough, neither did the wolf—it was far too interested in watching three friends play to worry about anything like that.

ψ

From a small window, a squeezing and hurrying man—with a huge bulging sack—jumped out into the night.

It was Rob the burglar. His shadow stretched long and far across the garden that was close to the house. Then it stretched up and over the fence that surrounded the garden and the house. It even stretched long and far across the wild garden towards the woods.

The wolf saw the shadow first; it stretched and touched his face. Then like a coiled spring, the wolf sprang. He flew through the air and landed right on top of Moonbeam and Lilybell with a squelchy thud.

String jumped with fright, and when noticing nothing was there, and after his heart had stopped pounding and his body had stopped shaking, he looked for his two friends.

Moonbeam and Lilybell were nowhere to be seen.

Rob the Burglar climbed over the fence and ran across the wild garden. It wasn't long before he reached where the wolf lay. There in the dark, with lots of puffing and panting, Rob the burglar rested. He couldn't see the wolf in the grass, but he could see two eyes of coal reflecting the moon.

String didn't move. His little legs wanted to run, but no matter how he willed them they refused to obey.

"What's this?" Rob the burglar questioned, snatching String.

Rob the burglar resembled a haystack with legs. He was extremely hairy and solidly built, but as bendable as rubber (and that's how something so big can manage to squeeze through such tiny windows). Despite his looks, he wouldn't hurt anything, not even a flea.

String dangled in Rob the burglar's hand and gave a little bark that sounded more like a squeak. Then he lost his enchantment and fell lifelessly to being just a knitted toy again.

"This might be worth something," Rob the burglar said, who started pressing String to make him squeak again, but couldn't. "That's once I get the squeaker fixed." Then opening the huge bulging sack he'd been carrying, he dropped String in.

Moonbeam and Lilybell could do nothing but watch from beneath an undetected wolf.

After a short rest, Rob the burglar and sack and stretching shadow headed off towards the woods.

The Wolf sprang up and ran as fast as it could towards the woods, casting his own shadow over Rob the burglar.

What happened next was painful...

Snap-bite went the jaws of the wolf.

"YEEAAOOOWWWW!" screamed Rob the burglar in terrible agony, and dropped the huge bulging sack.

The wolf's teeth sank deeper into the trousers of the burglar.

"GRRRRRR," growled the wolf from the side of its mouth, as it swung its head from side to side. The wolf's razor-sharp teeth almost met as the burglar's trousers ripped open to reveal a large bitten bottom.

Two naughty pixies had seen everything.

Tither

The owner of the house was Mr. Hedges. He'd been awakened by his creaking stairs and was now searching through every room for whoever had woken him.

It wasn't long before he found the open pantry window. A mouth-open Mr. Hedges wondered how anybody could have got through something so small. Nevertheless, they had and muddy footprints across the floor confirmed this.

This rubbery thief must be a giant, thought Mr. Hedges. *Those footprints are twice the size of mine.*

Mr. Hedges was a kind man with a big, round belly and when wide awake, was rather jolly. However, at this moment he was sleepy and very grumpy. He hated being disturbed in the night, especially when just a few moments ago he was as warm as toast in bed and dreaming of mounds of chocolate and toffee ice cream.

When Mr. Hedges was satisfied that no-one was in his house, he breathed a sigh of relief. It was then that he heard loud screams coming from outside.

Out through the front door of the house came two barrels of a gun, and gripping tightly to this gun was Mr. Hedges.

Mr. Hedges ran in the direction of the screaming; his big, round shadow pointing a long, thin shadow that stretched up to the wild garden. As Mr. Hedges ran, he didn't notice Moonbeam or Lilybell down in the grass. All he saw in the distance was a snap-biting wolf and a jumping giant.

"GET IT OFF ME! GET IT OFF ME!" screeched Rob the burglar.

The wolf bit down harder.

Rob the burglar screamed even louder, "YEEAAOOOWWWW!"

Moonbeam covered Lilybell's ears and hummed a song in his head, so that they didn't have to listen.

The wolf bit down harder.

The two-barrelled gun pointed into the distance.

BANG! BANG!

Smoke and sparks filled the air.

"YEEAAOOOWWWW!" screamed Rob the burglar, in even more pain.

"AW-ROOOOOOO," howled the wolf.

The huge, bulging sack dropped to the floor with a clinking and a clattering.

Rob the burglar ran off. He ran and ran as fast as his rubbery legs would take him, and not once did he look back.

The wolf however, didn't run. He lay on the ground not moving.

Soon Mr. Hedges was standing where the burglar stood and screamed, and the wolf had bitten and growled.

The gun was reloaded and was directed at the woods, ready to shoot again.

Nothing close to Mr. Hedges made a sound, but in the distance a howling of many wolves could be heard.

Mr. Hedges looked all around in the hope that the burglar had dropped whatever he'd stolen. It was then that he saw two things. Beside his feet was a little wolf and close by was the huge, bulging sack.

"Poor little wolf," Mr. Hedges said tearfully.

Then slinging the gun over his shoulder, he picked up the little wolf and the huge, bulging sack and returned to the house.

When the two naughty pixies finally lifted their bodies up from the grass, Mr. Hedges, the little wolf and the sack had disappeared.

Lilybell's golden hair stuck to her face in a frightful mess. Her powder-pink dress had lost all its silver sparkle, and her knees were as muddy as could be. None of this worried her. Her only concern was for her friend, String.

"Did you see what that nasty, hairy brute did?" she said angrily. "It's despicable, it's unthinkable, it's dislikeable, it's..."

"Horridable!" Moonbeam said.

"Yes, it would be if there was such a word," Lilybell said, "but you are right, it was horrible."

Moonbeam sulked at not been able to join in the something-able game.

"Did you see the giant go galloping into the woods?" he asked, cheering at the giant's misfortune. "And did you see his bitten and shot bare bum? Oops!" Moonbeam cried. "What if Ethelweard gets to hear about this?"

"Oh dear!" cried Lilybell.

"The man took the sack and the wolf to the house," Moonbeam said.

"What shall we do?" Lilybell asked. She looked towards the house, shuddered and quite rightly said, "If it wasn't for you foolishly leaving the woods, none of this would have happened."

"That wolf saved us," Moonbeam said, "and now the poor thing's dead."

Moonbeam felt so upset that he didn't care that his blue coat and yellow trousers were covered in mud. He didn't even care that his cherished snail-shell buttons were missing.

Mither

Mr. Hedges dropped the sack with a clink and a clatter on his kitchen floor. Then, with sadness, he gently rested the wolf's body on the kitchen table.

A small whimper came from the wolf as Mr. Hedges hung up his gun.

"You're still alive!" Mr. Hedges cried so happily that his heart felt like bursting into song. He smiled and wiped the tears from his eyes. "You lay still little wolf, and I'll take a look at your wounds."

And that's what Mr. Hedges did.

He carefully parted the blood-stained fur, and very slowly- with the aid of a pair of tweezers-removed lead pellets (that the two-barrelled gun had fired) from the wolf's skin. One by one the pellets dropped with a tinkle into a dish.

The night began to press its dark fingers onto Mr. Hedges' eyelids, but Mr. Hedges refused to doze off.

It was only when he was thoroughly satisfied that he had removed every last pellet, that he washed the little wolf's fur clean. It was now morning. The little wolf had been very brave and hadn't moved an inch.

Ψ

In the trees, birds were gossiping. All the twittering was about two odd mud-covered creatures. The subject was so interesting that their breakfast of lovely, wiggly worms hadn't been started.

ψ

Two naughty pixies followed their path deeper into the woods. It was nearly impossible to see them. Their mud-covered clothes seemed to camouflage them perfectly into their surroundings.

"I wonder what happened to that nasty, hairy brute?" Lilybell asked, looking around for any watching eyes.

"Hopefully he's been snap-bitten and eaten by the biggest, meanest wolf," Moonbeam said with a cruel grin. "He deserves it. What he did to poor String was horridable."

Lilybell didn't make any correction. However, she did think that to be snap-bitten and eaten by even the smallest of wolves must be very painful. Nobody, no matter what they'd done, deserved that.

ψ

Ethelweard was gathering brambles. His arms were raised as

high as could be; his fingers carefully picked the last of the autumn fruit.

Winter will soon be upon us, he thought.

Out of the corner of his eye he saw something move. He stretched his bramble-stained fingers in the direction of movement and said:

"Ash, Elm
be still."

Two naughty pixies instantly became trees.

Ethelweard carried on picking brambles as though nothing had happened.

"Little fools," he said. "There you will stay, until the passing of three day. A young wolf shot, teeth the burglar got, and String taken away."

Gossiping birds had told the wizard everything.

The Evergreen Wolf

Pip

Mr. Hedges laid the little wolf down by the fire to rest.

In half a minute the little wolf was asleep.

In another half-minute, Mr. Hedges was asleep—he'd sat in his comfy chair and happily dozed off.

ψ

In the woods, Moonbeam tried his hardest to move. No matter how hard he tried, his body refused—it didn't seem to belong to him anymore. He tried desperately to say something. His mind was shouting. Nothing escaped from a mouth of wood, not even a squeak.

Lilybell cried. No tears came from her eyes; instead they trickled down her throat. It was a horrible sensation. The feeling was as if a snake, made entirely of salt, was slithering towards her tummy. The taste was sickly.

ψ

Several hours passed and Mr. Hedges was waking and stretching, and wishing he hadn't fallen asleep in the chair. His neck had a crick in it.

"Ooh," he said, as his hand began rubbing the pain away.

The little wolf was also waking. It looked up at Mr. Hedges and gave a stretch and also whimpered in pain.

Poor thing! thought Mr. Hedges, who was just about to stroke the wolf and then thought better of it. "You just keep still while I get you something to eat," he said to the wolf.

Mr. Hedges wasn't stupid. This little wolf he'd helped was a wild animal, and wild animals bite (and we all heard the screams from Rob the burglar when he'd been snap-bitten). Mr. Hedges didn't want to end up like Rob the burglar.

The little wolf whimpered some more as a bowl of water and some bits of meat were carefully placed next to him.

"There's a good wolf," Mr. Hedges said with slight unease.

The young wolf moved its head and dipped its jaw into the water, and lapped up a cool drink.

Mr. Hedges watched and smiled.

ψ

Three days came and went, and the little wolf was feeling a lot better. Stretching seemed less painful.

Mr. Hedges made sure there was always fresh water and food nearby, and carried on as normal. Well, as normal as could be when a wolf is in your house.

ψ

In the woods, Ethelweard was watching two trees.

Moonbeam's legs turned to wibbly jelly as all feeling of being Moonbeam slowly returned. He slumped to his knees sobbing.

Lilybell's legs turned to wobbly jelly as all feeling of being Lilybell slowly returned. She slumped to her knees beside Moonbeam, but she didn't cry.

"String has been taken," Moonbeam blubbered.

"I know," Ethelweard said, giving Moonbeam a very unpleasing and penetrating stare.

"Is he..." Moonbeam started to say.

"He's nothing!" Ethelweard said crossly. "He's just a knitted toy again; he was touched by Rob the burglar."

"Oh! How is Rob?" Lilybell asked timidly.

The wizard gave a worried look and thought hard about the enchanted spell he'd cast over String.

"You should ask the wolves that," he said harshly, then added in a much softer tone, "but I wouldn't if I were you. Protection from a wolf bite can only last seven times, after that it's hello to razor-sharp teeth."

Lilybell trembled and said nothing more about Rob the burglar.

"YOU ARE THE TWO NAUGHTIEST PIXIES EVER," Ethelweard's scolding was so loud that his voice bounced from tree to tree. "YOU'VE BEEN OUT OF THE WOODS' PROTECTION AND YOU WERE SEEN. YOU STUPID FOOLS." The wizard was so mad he began to go as purple as a bramble.

Moonbeam and Lilybell's red faces became ghostly pale as they looked to the ground in shame. They didn't dare say anything back.

"Now I don't want to hear any more about String or Rob the burglar," Ethelweard said, quietening his voice so only the nearest tree could hear. "The wolves are angry enough about losing one from their pack. I'm just glad we didn't lose two from ours," he said more warmly. Not another word on the subject was said as he turned and walked away muttering, "You look filthy. Go away and get washed. Change into something more in keeping with the time of year. And for goodness sake... stay out of trouble."

Teaser

Lilybell felt saddened.

"I didn't start the trouble," stated Moonbeam.

"I know," Lilybell said. Then dropping her voice to a whisper said, "It was Rob the burglar."

"Precisely," agreed Moonbeam. "Just look at the mess he's caused. I've been a tree for three days and my legs feel like jelly."

"You should be thinking about how to get String back and explaining things to the wolves," Lilybell said, surprised at Moonbeam's selfishness.

"Are you stark raving mad?" Moonbeam cried. "What do you think the wolves would do to me?"

"Well, at least you can go and get String back," Lilybell said, adamant that all the trouble they were in wasn't her fault.

ψ

Moonbeam sat and thought.

"A rescue won't be easy," he said. He was feeling brave again, in a foolish way.

"Won't it?" Lilybell asked, with a twinkle in her eye.

"No, it'll be dangerous". A beaming smile, that gave Moonbeam his name, spread wide with mischief.

"Have you got a plan?" Lilybell asked.

"Not yet," Moonbeam said, "but I soon will have." He started to walk and as he walked, he thought. But all he could think about was being a tree for possibly hundreds of days, followed by a far more serious telling off.

Lilybell followed Moonbeam.

Soon they were nearing the other end of the woods.

The woods' leaf-canopied roof grew thinner. Sunlight filtered gently to the ground.

Moonbeam came to an abrupt halt. He could hear someone talking, and wolves growling.

Lilybell heard it too. She didn't stop and bumped into Moonbeam.

Moonbeam put his finger across his lips, suggesting quietness.

"Who is it?" Lilybell said under her breath; her eyes darted from shadow to shadow and from tree to tree.

The only thing that these two daring pixies could do was to be as quiet as mice.

Moonbeam got as close as he could possibly get without being seen. Lilybell followed.

Moonbeam inched a little close and foolishly tripped over a tree root-he nearly choked as he fell.

Lilybell gasped in horror as countless wolves' eyes stared in their direction. She quickly lay down next to Moonbeam.

"AWHOOOOO!" howled a wolf.

"AWHOOOOO!" howled another wolf.

"Shut up!" Rob the burglar scolded. "There's no one there who can help you."

And indeed it looked exactly as the burglar said. Moonbeam and Lilybell were so mud-covered that they just merged into the woods' leaf-strewn ground.

Now all eyes were back on Rob the burglar.

"I dare you to try and eat me again," Rob the burglar taunted. He held a large stick in one hand while his other covered his bare bum. "If you do I'll knock more of your teeth out," he said, as he swirled the stick around at a tremendous pace.

The wolves watched and wondered what to do.

"Look!" whispered Lilybell. "Three of the wolves have lost all their teeth."

Moonbeam saw that three of the wolves had indeed lost their teeth–a scattering of cracked and shattered teeth lay on the ground.

"Look!" whispered Lilybell. "That wolf has bleeding paws."

Moonbeam saw a wolf with bleeding paws that had snapped and splintered claws.

Then, without warning, two brave wolves leapt through the air at Rob the burglar.

The stick swung and missed.

Snap-bite went the wolves' jaws.

Rob the burglar felt nothing but a tickle and laughed.

Suddenly, the air cracked and sparked fire.

"**AW-ROOOOOOO,**" howled the two wolves, as their tails burst into flame. They puffed and blew on their tails, but the fire kept on burning. They wiped and rubbed their tails into the ground, but the fire kept on burning. When there was no more tail to burn, the fire went out. Two sad-looking wolves sat and whimpered.

"Ethelweard would be proud of that," Lilybell hinted.

"Rob the burglar must have taken String's protection," murmured Moonbeam, understanding what he was seeing.

"And he's only got one protection left," Lilybell hinted.

Moonbeam agreed and mouthed, "But the wolves don't know that."

Then, one by one, the wolves left. And so did Rob the burglar. He ran and ran and ran out of the woods.

"Do you think we'll ever see him again?" Lilybell asked.

"Not blooming likely," Moonbeam said, laughing so hard his belly hurt.

Leaser

As each day passed, the little wolf grew stronger. Mr. Hedges chopped firewood for the coming winter and secured his home from burglars. He also tidied the shed and put a flap in its door. It was time for the little wolf to be independent again.

Mr. Hedges took some food and water into the shed and placed them next to a blanket. The little wolf followed him into the shed and sniffed and sniffed and sniffed.

Mr. Hedges left the little wolf and returned to the house. Every so often, he would go and see the little wolf and take him more food.

"I'll be going away for a few days," he said to the little wolf.

It was because the little wolf was getting stronger that Mr. Hedges went to visit his godson.

ψ

Things were happening in the woods. The north wind brought the cold. The trees lost all their leaves, and the wolves changed their colour. Two naughty pixies also changed their appearance. They dressed in brown and copper to merge in with their surroundings.

The first frosts came and covered everything in sparkling jewels. When a wolf was seen, it looked grey and statue-like.

L. Sydney Abel

Moonbeam continued to think of a plan to rescue String. The more he thought, the more the word 'trouble' began to write itself across his face. His suggestion was to do what Rob the burglar did and break into the house.

Lilybell approved the plan.

"I'm coming with you," she said.

"Of course you are," agreed Moonbeam, "you're my look-out."

ψ

That night, the sky was clear and the ground was as hard as a skeleton's backbone. Frost covered everything the eye could see. The wild garden sparkled in the moon's light, making Lilybell feel slightly jealous of its beauty.

"Come on," Moonbeam called, as he crunched his way over the brittle grass.

"Isn't everything so pretty?" Lilybell said.

"Including the grey wolves that might be watching us?" Moonbeam asked, glancing back with fear.

It was difficult to know if the wolves were there or not, everything looked grey.

Lilybell glanced over her shoulder and shuddered.

"It's just awful to think that those beastly animals want to eat us," she said, running to catch up.

"Not all wanted to eat us," Moonbeam said, "remember?"

Lilybell remembered and felt very ashamed of her thoughts.

Over the fence they both climbed, and across the garden they both ran. Soon they were hidden amongst the plants that grew beneath the windows of the house.

"Now what?" Lilybell panted, with white breath.

"I look through the window," murmured Moonbeam, standing on tiptoe and gripping the window sill. Then with a sharp pull, he hoisted himself up. "I can't see String through this window," he whispered. "Let's try another."

Moonbeam looked through all the downstairs windows, but String was nowhere to be seen.

"Maybe he's upstairs," Lilybell suggested.

"I'll go and see," murmured Moonbeam.

"Only spiders can climb walls to see through upstairs windows," whispered Lilybell. "I'm frightened you might fall."

"You are silly," murmured Moonbeam. "I'm not going to climb the wall. I'm going to be like Rob the burglar and climb the stairs."

Moonbeam tried to open the downstairs windows. They wouldn't open. Every window, including the small pantry one, had a lock fitted to it. Mr. Hedges had been busy.

Catra

The two naughty pixies looked for a way into the house.

There was only a tiny gap under the door, just right for a mouse to squeeze under.

"That's it," whispered Lilybell, feeling she had the answer.

"What is?" murmured Moonbeam. His round face suddenly got curiously much rounder.

"If you were a mouse you could squeeze under the door," whispered Lilybell, with a naughty smile. She pointed at Moonbeam and quietly repeated an incantation she'd heard:

> "Pointy nose and tiny toes and tail long,
> a mouse you will be if I'm not wrong.
> Only seconds it will last
> before you return as you were in the past."

"A mouse..." Moonbeam started to say, but that's as far as he got before his face grew long and his cheeks burst whiskers. "Help me, eek, eek, eek," he cried, as he shrank. His high pitched squeaking could be heard as his bones crunched and cracked.

A tail grew as Moonbeam transformed into exactly what Lilybell had turned him into-a tiny mouse.

"Quickly," she instructed, pointing to the gap under the door.

The mouse looked sparkly-eyed. Then as flat as a postal letter it slipped under the door. And just in time, because as soon as its tail disappeared from Lilybell's view, the mouse became Moonbeam again.

"That was horrid," murmured Moonbeam, looking at his bottom to make sure the tail had completely gone. "My nose won't stop twitching," he complained, "and how did you learn to do that?"

Lilybell giggled.

"I once saw Ethelweard do it when he locked himself out," she whispered. "I thought it was terrifically clever."

"Why didn't he just command the door to open?" murmured Moonbeam, feeling his round face for any last trace of whiskers.

"Maybe he likes being a mouse," whispered Lilybell, giggling some more.

"Well I don't," muttered Moonbeam, on finding that his ears were still mouse-shaped and furry. "Oh bother," he muttered grumpily.

"Go and find String," instructed Lilybell.

Moonbeam didn't argue because that was why he was here, but he still didn't like being told what to do and especially by Lilybell.

Up the stairs climbed Moonbeam.

When he reached the top, his ears were his own again. He looked in the bedrooms–String wasn't there. He even looked in the bathroom, peeping with one eye, just in case–String wasn't there either.

Down the banister slid Moonbeam.

"He's not here," he told Lilybell.

"Have you looked everywhere?" she asked.

"Yes, everywhere," confirmed Moonbeam. "Even the man who brought him here isn't here."

"He's not?" Lilybell questioned. She pointed to herself and said:

"Pointy nose and tiny toes and tail long,

a mouse you will be if I'm not wrong.

Only seconds it will last

before you return as you were in the past."

A few seconds later and Lilybell was standing next to Moonbeam.

"You don't believe me, do you?" Moonbeam asked, watching Lilybell wiggle her nose and check to see if the tail had gone.

"Don't be silly," said Lilybell. "I just wanted to have a nosey around."

Lilybell climbed the stairs. Moonbeam followed. When they reached the top, Lilybell searched for String.

String wasn't upstairs.

"He could be hidden downstairs," Lilybell suggested.

"Follow me," Moonbeam said. He slid down the banister again.

Lilybell followed, and was soon searching the downstairs rooms.

"He's not here," Lilybell said, looking extremely disappointed.

"I told you that," Moonbeam snapped.

Lilybell was just about to say the mouse spell again, when scratching was heard at the door.

"AWHOOOOO!" howled the little wolf.

CLICK went the lock.

Horna

Moonbeam felt terrified-his knees knocked together.

"Do something!" he cried.

"Like what?" Lilybell asked.

"Anything!" Moonbeam cried.

But there wasn't time.

The door handle turned. The door creaked open. In walked Mr. Hedges. The little wolf was at his heels, sniff, sniff, sniffing.

"What have we here?" Mr. Hedges questioned, quickly shutting the door. "Two robbers, caught red-handed," he sneered.

"Our hands aren't red," Moonbeam said, turning his trembling hands over so Mr. Hedges could see. "We're not robbers," he said truthfully.

"THEN WHAT ARE YOU?" Mr. Hedges shouted.

Lilybell couldn't stop herself from crying. She began gulping on salty tears.

Moonbeam thought it looked better if he supported Lilybell by doing the same. He also started to cry. Huge floods of tears fell from his honest screwed-up eyes and sploshed onto the floor.

"Wahh, wahh, wahh," wailed Lilybell and Moonbeam.

"Wahhooo, wahhooo, wahhooo," howled the little wolf, giving his support.

"I'm sorry I shouted," Mr. Hedges said. "I thought I was being robbed again." It was then that he understood who he was talking to and stared in astonishment at those he didn't believe in.

"We're in big trouble," Moonbeam said, looking directly into Lilybell's frightened eyes. "Do the mouse thing."

"The wolf is by the door," Lilybell explained. "He eats mice."

"Oh, I didn't think of that," Moonbeam said. "Can't you turn the man into a mouse, so the wolf can eat him?"

"No," Lilybell replied.

"Should we cry again?" Moonbeam suggested.

"Not again," Lilybell said. "It'll be much better if we tell the truth."

"Oh dear," Moonbeam said. "That'll make even bigger trouble. If we ever get out of here I'll be a tree for years."

When Mr. Hedges saw Lilybell's frightened eyes, he bent down and whispered, "Don't be afraid, I won't hurt you."

To prove he meant it, he made a roaring fire that lit the room with warmth. He took out of his travelling bag a fruit cake and a bottle of fizzy lemonade. "Let's have something to eat and drink," he said softly, cutting the cake and pouring three glasses of fizz.

In a comfy chair sat Mr. Hedges. Next to the fire sat the little wolf. Between them sat Moonbeam and Lilybell, each with a piece of cake and a thimble of lemonade.

ψ

Moonbeam liked fizzy lemonade. It made his tummy bubble, and made him whistle every time he burped.

Lilybell explained who they were and where they were from.

Moonbeam said nothing. He thought the less he said, the less time he would spend as a tree.

Lilybell also told about the wild garden and about Rob the burglar. She described how the little wolf saved them and how they lost String. They believed the little wolf had died.

"He's as good as new," Mr. Hedges said proudly, looking at the little wolf.

"He's evergreen," whispered Moonbeam, into Lilybell's ear.

Mr. Hedges frowned at Moonbeam.

"'He's evergreen'," Lilybell repeated.

"Evergreen! What do you mean?"

"It means that he's been touched by Man, and so can't change colour," Lilybell said.

Mr. Hedges looked confused. "What colour should he be?"

"He becomes grey with the frosts and white with the snow," Lilybell declared.

"What will happen if he doesn't change colour?"

Moonbeam whispered into Lilybell's ear again.

"What did he say?" Mr. Hedges asked.

"'Hiss, hiss, hiss'," Lilybell repeated.

Mr. Hedges looked even more confused.

"He was speaking so quickly I couldn't hear what he said," Lilybell admitted.

Moonbeam's face turned red.

"I believe the little wolf will be rejected by the other wolves," Lilybell confessed.

"I believe you're right about that," Mr. Hedges said.

Moonbeam's face thundered.

"Tell me about your friend String." requested Mr. Hedges.

Lilybell explained.

Dick

Mr. Hedges listened and understood. He had a confession.

"String was here, but he isn't anymore," he said. "He's with my godson; he's his knitted dog called Wuffy.

"No, he's String," Moonbeam said sternly, forgetting all about becoming a tree.

"No, he's Wuffy," Mr. Hedges said firmly. "He was Wuffy long before he was String."

Moonbeam pursed his lips and scowled.

Lilybell wanted to know how long her friend would be away. "He will come back, won't he?" she asked, her eyes sparkling new tears.

"Of course he will," Mr. Hedges said. "As my godson grows up his need for Wuffy will lessen."

Moonbeam whispered into Lilybell's ear.

"'When will that be?'" Lilybell repeated.

Mr. Hedges thought and then said, "About five winters more."

"Poor String," Lilybell said.

"You're forgetting that he's not magical anymore," Mr. Hedges said. "He doesn't feel or think anything."

"That'll be me when Ethelweard hears about this," mumbled Moonbeam.

Lilybell agreed. "Yes, I'll say it was all your idea and that I only came along to try and keep you out of trouble." she said, smiling.

Mr. Hedges also smiled. He knew Lilybell was only teasing. "When the time comes, I'll bring your friend back," he promised.

ψ

In the woods, wolves huddled together. They looked like weathered concrete, rock-solid against the cold north wind.

The wind blow stronger, bringing snow.

By morning the wind had gone, but not the snow. The ground had a carpet of white. Bare trees stretched up into a white sky.

ψ

Mr. Hedges was asleep. His chest rose up and down with his breathing.

Moonbeam cringed at Mr. Hedges' night-long snore with its habitual snort.

The little wolf was asleep. He seemed to copy Mr. Hedges by making a night-long snuffle with an annoying wheeze.

The only one to sleep soundly was Lilybell. She was too pretty to snore, snort, snuffle or wheeze.

Moonbeam hadn't had a wink's sleep. He was grumpy and desperately wanted to pinch Lilybell awake, but he didn't. He just sat there with his arms crossed.

Mr. Hedges gave a yawn and stretched and wished he hadn't fallen asleep in the chair–he'd got another crick in his neck.

Moonbeam secretly smiled at seeing Mr. Hedges frantically rub his neck free from pain.

The little wolf also stretched and yawned. He was obviously in no pain because he started scratching his ear with his back leg.

Lilybell woke with a start, and immediately sat upright.

"Oh my!" she said. "Are we still here? What time is it? Hadn't we better be going?"

"Unfortunately... morning... and yes," answered Moonbeam all at once.

Mr. Hedges looked at the little wolf. "It's time for you to go," he said. "You should go see the wizard. Lilybell will explain things."

The little wolf came up close to Mr. Hedges, and rubbed his nose into his hand.

Mr. Hedges stroked the little wolf's head. "Go freely and safely," he said, as a small tear blurred his vision. He opened the door to a land white with winter.

"You won't forget your promise?" Lilybell said.

"I won't," Mr. Hedges said.

The little wolf ran across the garden and over the fence, leaving tracks in the snow as he went. At the wild garden he waited for Moonbeam and Lilybell to catch up.

All three looked back to see Mr. Hedges waving goodbye. Then they walked side-by-side towards the woods.

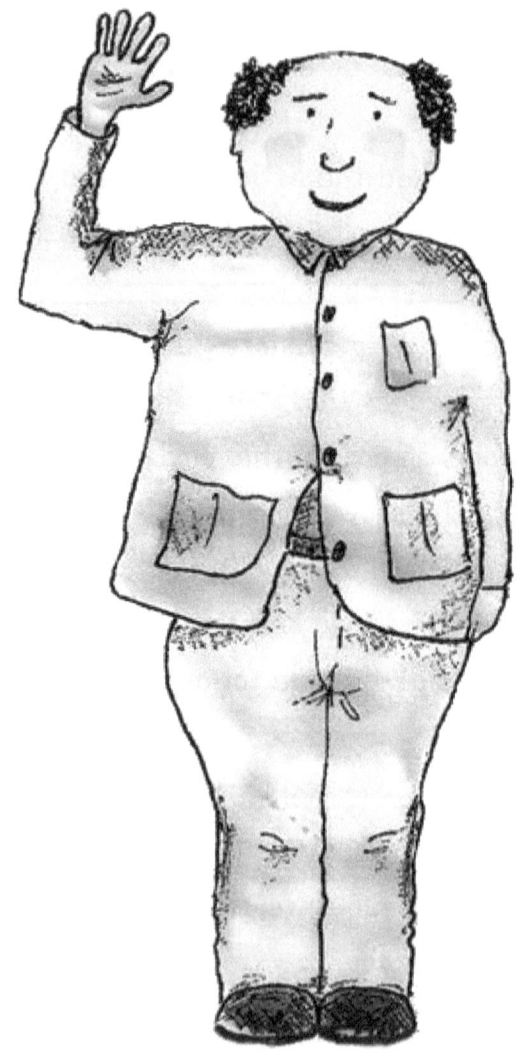

Ψ

From the woods walked the wizard. At first he was pleased to see the pixies, but when he saw their tracks coming from the house he was angry.

When the little wolf, Moonbeam and Lilybell saw how angry the wizard looked, their hearts almost stopped from fear.

"It's bad enough that you've been away all night," Ethelweard scolded, "but to be with a human is UNFORGIVABLE."

The trees behind the wizard shook so nervously that snow fell from their branches.

"I'm going to be a tree for years," boohooed Moonbeam.

"Maybe not years," Ethelweard said, looking at the little wolf.

"He's evergreen," Lilybell said. "Can you help him?"

"That," Ethelweard began, "will not be easy. To remove the touch of Man, and restore his gift, will take great magic."

"Please try," Lilybell begged.

Moonbeam didn't say a word. He knew whatever he said would never change what the wizard thought about him. Trouble was trouble and he was three daffodils high in it.

Yan-dick

Like shadows, statues of grey came from the woods.

Advancing paw after advancing paw crept closer, until the grey wolves were only yards away from Ethelweard, Lilybell, Moonbeam and the little wolf.

"WEHAVEYOUUUU!" howled the leading grey wolf.

The grey wolves slowly and silently circled their prey.

It was too late for anyone to run.

"Blast and be bothered, fiddle-de-dee, I'm a fool as he is next to me," said Ethelweard, glaring at Moonbeam for making him break his own rule.

The wolves' snarled-drooling jaws showed razor-sharp teeth.

"Oh my, this is going to hurt," Moonbeam said.

"FO-OOOOOOD!" howled all the wolves, closing in tighter.

Moonbeam held Lilybell tight.

Ethelweard drew his arms into the air...

BANG! BANG!

Smoke and tiny white-hot sparks, which sizzled in the ice-cold air, sent lead pellets flying over scared heads.

"AHH-WOOOOOOO!" howled all the grey wolves. And running as fast as they could, with their tails between their legs thinking they might catch fire, they vanished into the woods.

Moonbeam and Lilybell felt terrified–their knees knocked together.

The little wolf cowered.

"How did I do that?" Ethelweard asked.

"You didn't," Moonbeam said.

Mr. Hedges stood behind his fence and waved.

"HOORAY," shouted Moonbeam and Lilybell.

The little wolf wagged his tail.

Ethelweard merely bowed ever so politely.

ψ

The wizard led the way back to the woods. More snow began to fall; it covered the already white ground so quickly that their footsteps soon became lost.

"We need to shelter," Ethelweard said.

"Good," Moonbeam said, and shivered.

Lilybell was so cold her teeth chattered.

The little wolf didn't complain. He liked the snow, even if he was the wrong colour.

When they were safe inside the wizard's home, Ethelweard began looking through his ancient book of magic.

ψ

Days passed and still the wizard hadn't found what he was looking for.

Outside it had stopped snowing. As far as the eye could see was a deep carpet of white.

The snow told the wolves it was time to leave.

One by one, a white wolf left the woods and climbed the neighbouring hills to higher ground. There they would be safe from any guns. It was too cold and dangerous for Man to go looking for wolves in winter, especially when they couldn't be seen.

Tean-dick

"EUREKA!" screamed the wizard.

Moonbeam, who was napping, fell off his chair.

The little wolf ran around excitedly.

Lilybell clapped for joy.

"Now," Ethelweard said, "we can begin."

The wizard drew the sleeves of his robe around himself and engulfed the little wolf within. Something was said, then wizard and wolf were gone.

ψ

In the centre of the woods was a clearing. This was where serious magic was done.

The wizard stood with his arms outstretched, swirling the air.

The little wolf hid under the wizard's robe and waited.

Ethelweard called out to the sky:

"Silver star from afar,
remove the touch of man.

The Evergreen Wolf

Whitest light to blackness flight,
evergreen be gone."

The wind blew and the snow spiralled, and still Ethelweard stood with his arms outstretched.

Suddenly, the sky flashed silver; thunder shook the ground.

The wizard snatched the sky above his head.

He called to the ground:

"Colour fade from masquerade,
disappear into the earth.
Pure white from star bright,
begin as if from birth."

The wind stopped blowing and the snow ceased to fall. Ethelweard lowered his arms. The little wolf came out from under the wizard's robe.

The wizard sprinkled silver star-light over the little wolf.

The little wolf began to run around. Slowly his camouflage of summer turned to grey.

"AWHOOOOO!" howled the little wolf.

Soon the little wolf was nowhere to be seen.

ψ

All the pixies of the woods came to see why the wind had spiralled and why the sky suddenly flashed and thundered.

"Where is the little wolf?" Moonbeam asked.

"Did you help him?" Lilybell asked.

Ethelweard smiled and said, "Can you see him?"

Everyone shook their head.

"Then I must have helped him," Ethelweard said.

The wizard led everyone to the edge of the woods that faced the hills.

"Be with your own kind," Ethelweard instructed the whitest little wolf.

Under a white sky, wolf tracks could be seen to climb the white hills.

Now whether the little wolf turned to say goodbye, no one knew.

"AWHOOOOO!" came from the hills.

"Thank you," Lilybell said.

The wizard didn't say anything; he never took praise for the things he did. But he did give Moonbeam a knowing look as he turned and walked back to the clearing in the centre of the woods.

There he counted the pixies. "Yan, tean, tither, mither, pip..."

When every pixie was counted and gathered in a circle, it was time.

"It is now WE that should be unseen," Ethelweard said, calling to the earth for its protection. "WE shall become like the woods and sleep until spring."

"But I don't want to sleep until spring," Moonbeam said.

Ethelweard explained, "The woods in winter are where Man comes and cuts the season's traditions. "I will become a tree, and you will become mistletoe. Man doesn't cut down the tree which the mistletoe grows on. He only cuts off a sprig of mistletoe that bares the berry."

"What for?" Lilybell asked.

"Kisses!" answered Ethelweard.

Lilybell liked the sound of that. She gave Moonbeam a sheepish smile.

Moonbeam smiled awkwardly. His round face turned bright red.

"What will happen if Man cuts off my berries?" Moonbeam asked.

"Nothing," answered Ethelweard. "It's just like having your hair cut." The wizard spread his fingers upon the ground and spoke magic:

"A silver birch for all to see,
my branches support a secret life.
Traditions are feeding from me,
winter kisses will bring forth a wife.
Secrets keep while we sleep,
until the earth warms and rejoices.
Where spring's new life begins to peep,
and hear again our voices."

The snow swirled and rose again as the wizard's voice dug deep into the earth.

When the snow stopped falling, a tall silver birch stood still and silent. Snuggling and sleeping within its branches hung mistletoe.

White berries sparkled, ready to become winter's kisses.

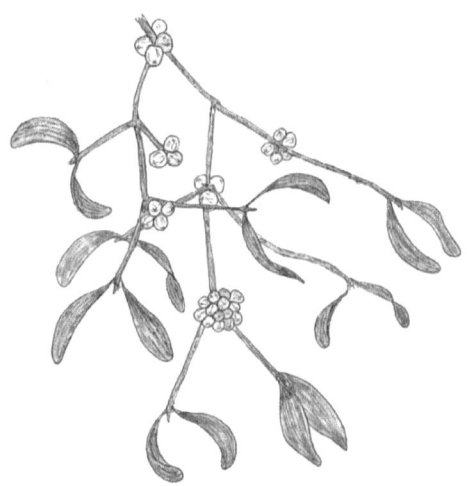

ψ

Mr. Hedges decorated a tree with coloured baubles and stood it by his front door. Inside, he pinned sprigs of mistletoe to the hall ceiling and crossed his fingers. Then he looked through the window to the hills and knew he would never see the little wolf again.

The ending

A note:

Did you know that Mr. Hedges was my godfather?

You didn't! Well now you do.

My godfather, Humph as I knew him, was correct in his foretelling of five winters more. It was when I turned ten that I no longer played with Wuffy (or String as you know him).

When Humph told me this story, I had no reason to disbelieve him so I gave him String willingly. I never saw him return String to his friends. He did say however, that Lilybell told him about the mistletoe magic and that one day he would find a wife.

Did that winter's kiss, you might ask, come true?

Yes it did, but that's another story!

Humph, looking very young and smart

How did Gruvel come to be on the Gregorys' doorstep?

Where has Gruvel come from?

And what on earth are they going to do with Gruvel?

As the family try to answer these questions,
Gruvel teaches them a wonderful lesson.

For more information
visit: www.speakingvolumes.us

One morning, whilst getting out of bed, a voice
whispered the name 'Kingsley Trunk' into my ear.
I always pay attention to my whisperer,
whoever that may be…

Written and Illustrated by
L. Sydney Abel

For more information
visit: www.speakingvolumes.us

I'd like to go back in time, to put hurtful wrongs to right.
My advice: make time for the ones you love

A donkey, a letter, and a bottle of clear liquid
all combine to make 'The Secret'.

For more information
visit: www.speakingvolumes.us

One evening, my whisperer said the name 'Arthur Runkin'.
My imagination was alight!

Imagine knowing something about yourself.
And all because of a suitcase.

For more information
visit: www.speakingvolumes.us

The story unfolds alongside a catchy rhyme
and delightful illustrations as Patrick
goes on a journey of discovery.

For more information
visit: www.speakingvolumes.us

**Daydreaming about pirate adventures transports
'Then' to 'Now'**

**Sleepin' be one thing an' dreamin' be another.
But when dreamin' walks into yer wakin'
then that be something altogether diff'rent.**

For more information
visit: www.speakingvolumes.us

Under Nelida Wellington's stairs lives a Jinny-Yen.
Only children can see such creatures.
A Jinny-Yen is a Wish Granter.

And for most boys and girls, their thoughts turn to greed.
But not all children are devoured by greed...

For more information
visit: www.speakingvolumes.us

www.ingramcontent.com/pod-product-compliance
Lightning Source LLC
Chambersburg PA
CBHW030539180626
46810CB00005B/1939